Daredevil the Cat

Written by
Zhang Qiusheng

Illustrated by
Wu Bo

CARDINAL
MEDIA

Daredevil the cat lived in a very fine forest. He loved dangerous adventures and lived rather recklessly, all because he'd heard cats have nine lives.

Daredevil even chose eight more names
in case he should need them:
Stealth
Whisker Risker
Breakneck
Fearless Feline
Hazard Finder
Dauntless
Justin Time
Danger Cat

Daredevil should have checked his cat
facts more closely.

One day, the rain pelted down. While Daredevil liked adventure, he didn't like to get wet, so he opened his umbrella and set off.

Soon the rain stopped, the sun came out, and the sky looked as blue as the ocean.

"What a beautiful sky. What fresh air. I should be flying up there!" Daredevil said.

Daredevil couldn't actually fly, but he could swing. He swooped back and forth and went higher and higher. As the wind whistled past his ears, Daredevil heard a little chipmunk call, "Cat! It's too dangerous! You'll fall right off that swing!"

"Haven't you heard?
Cats have nine lives!"
Daredevil called out as
he let go and flew off.

As Daredevil sailed into the air, he thought he heard the chipmunk calling after him, "It's not true that cats have nine lives!" Daredevil kept soaring on, thinking he must not have heard the chipmunk quite right.

As Daredevil flew over the pine forest, a tall tree called out, "Cat! Grab a branch! I'll help you down!"

But Daredevil bounced off its branches like a trampoline, which made him fly even higher and even faster. "No thanks! Cats have nine lives!" Daredevil cried.

The pine tree shook his branches at this foolishness and yelled, "No they don't!"

As Daredevil soared away, he wondered, "What did that tree say?"

A gorilla in the silver birch forest saw Daredevil
fly over the trees and called out, 'Cat! I'll catch you
with my book!' But Daredevil bounced off its pages,
springing even higher in the sky and calling,
"Don't bother! Cats have nine lives!"

Daredevil thought he heard the gorilla call after him,
"This book says that's a myth!"

The gorilla shook her head at Daredevil's recklessness.

Daredevil flew past the forest and the mountain peaks. He soared so far and so high, there weren't even any chipmunks…

…or trees.

…or gorillas.

Suddenly Daredevil felt very scared. He finally understood what the chipmunk and the tree and the gorilla had been trying to tell him. Now he realized he was about to be smashed into a thousand pieces! Why had he been so reckless with this one life of his?

Daredevil began to fall. As he dropped to the ground, he was trembling and crying and sobbing. How had he been so foolish?

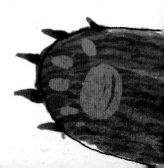

On a little hill, a little sheep was enjoying the sun.

One of Daredevil's tears dropped onto her nose.
The sheep lifted her head and said, "Is it
raining again? And is that little black
cloud holding an umbrella?"

Daredevil heard the sheep and remembered—
his umbrella! He popped it open and began to
float down.

"That little black cloud *is* holding an umbrella!"
said the sheep.

But just then the umbrella gave out. Daredevil stopped floating and started falling again.

Help! Help!

"Help! Help!" he called. "Cats only have one life!"

Thwack! Daredevil landed
on the tower of a castle
and began to slide down
its smooth side.

Daredevil tumbled into the royal garden where the king, the queen, and the prince had watched him slide down the castle tower.

The king demanded, "Tell me why I shouldn't punish you for sliding down my castle!"

Daredevil said, "I have been foolish and reckless, your majesty, but today I have learned a great lesson about how precious life is."

The king realized that Daredevil could be a valuable teacher for his son, so he invited the cat to join them in the castle.

"Thank you, your majesty!" Daredevil said.

Daredevil became the young prince's teacher and friend. Under Daredevil's guidance, the prince learned to value his own life and the lives of all people in the kingdom. He became a great king.

Many years passed. As Daredevil grew older, he missed his fine forest. One day he asked the king if he could return home.

The king agreed. "You have taught me well,
old friend," he said. "Even though I will miss
you, I wish for you to live out your life happily."

It's said that an old
black cat still lives in
that forest, enjoying
his one (very long) life.